for my son - love is everywhere you are, because you are love.

and, as always, for my mom & her boundless energy.

energy never leaves us, it only transforms

everywhere, and in my heart
© hannah alley 2020
All rights reserved.

book design by hannah alley
printed in the United States of America

written march 22, 2017

everywhere,
and in my heart

written by hannah alley
watercolor by jenna hubbard

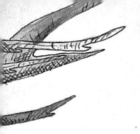

hey, it's been a while,

like forever and a day,

but in my heart

i know you're with me

every step of the way.

you're with the birds -

high in the sky,

flying free,

reminding me

it's ok

to just be.

there you are

dancing,

having fun,

bouncing in the shadows

of a setting sun.

on a blushing moon

rising high

you're everywhere,

just like the sky.

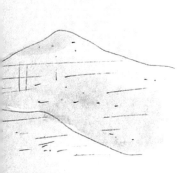

dontcha know

you're the grooviest tune.

i feel you flow

sometimes all afternoon.

when music plays,

there's no delay,

my fingers snap

and my body sways.

anywhere there's laughter

and everywhere there's fun...

you're easily found

in all the sweet moments

just *buzzing* around.

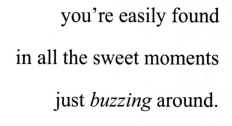

you're the whistle of a wren

singing high on the breeze.

like a curve in the wind -

you go just as you please.

it takes just one song,

played on soft summer leaves,

to remind me

i'm right where i belong.

you're the night sky -
glistening with stars that shine
like the light in your eyes
reminding me, love can fly.

if ever that glow grows dim
you're there to show me,
love can always be found
if i just look within.

your love has been with me

since the day I was born,

it won't ever leave me,

it only transforms.

so, i let you flow always

and watch love take form.

you're everywhere.

everywhere, and in my heart.

the end

and the beginning

grounding

Find yourself a comfortable seated position.
Allow your gaze to soften as you
audibly exhale all the air from your lungs.
Inhale deeply through your nose.
Good.

Do that 5 more times.

Witness your breath as it expands every cell. Bring awareness
to the stillness between each breath. What happens there?

a love letter to the reader

I came to *everywhere, in my heart* after the death of my mom.
In this nonlinear journey with grief, I've become intimate with
its power to re-connect us deeply to ourselves
and the natural world.

When I surrendered to the unforgiving waves of grief,
allowing myself to move with instead of against them,
I experienced a cathartic release. Poetry poured out from within,
death gave way to life, and this story was born.
Death is always incubating new life waiting to unfold.

*This story represents the alchemy of grief
and the transformative power of love.*

This story also carries deep reverence for the
boundless capacity for love.

The rest of these pages belong to you and yours,
in no particular order.
My desire is that you use them to feel deeply, share what's heavy on
your heart, and let the waves of grief usher you to new shores.
There are always new shores to discover.

Remember love is everywhere, and in your heart.

deep love,
hannah

so long as we love, we grieve.
and grief, I've found, comes in waves.

Imagine you're standing in front of a large ocean wave. Release the urge to tense up in preparation to fight the wave; instead, relax and surrender to it. In doing so, you'll find you can actually ride over it.

Try it.

Embrace the waves of grief as they roll up.

What do you feel?
Allow yourself to feel fully.
(draw, write, or dream)

deep healing comes from
feeling fully and without apology.

This page is just for you to feel all of it, *especially the pain.*

What hurts?
(draw, write, or dream)

from the deep pain of grief we begin to recognize the magic of everyday life, seeing it in things we have previously been blind to.

So love, like we read in the book, can take on many forms.

**Name all the different ways
love shows up in your life.**
(draw, write, or dream)

when we alchemize the life force of grief,
which has the power to break our heart,
it turns into fuel for the soul
to be shared freely with the world.

How can you alchemize your grief today?
(draw, write, or dream)

love is everywhere,

and in your heart

Made in the USA
Middletown, DE
07 December 2022

16746935R00022